# Off to First Grade

## ALSO BY LOUISE BORDEN

*The Last Day of School*

*The Little Ships: The Heroic Rescue at Dunkirk in World War II*

*Good-bye, Charles Lindbergh*

*Good Luck, Mrs. K.!*

*Sleds on Boston Common: A Story from the American Revolution*

*Fly High!: The Story of Bessie Coleman*

*The Day Eddie Met the Author*

*America Is . . .*

*Touching the Sky: The Flying Adventures of Wilbur and Orville Wright*

*Sea Clocks: The Story of Longitude*

*The A+ Custodian*

*The Greatest Skating Race: A World War II Story from the Netherlands*

*The John Hancock Club*

*The Lost-and-Found Tooth*

•

MARGARET K. McELDERRY BOOKS

# Louise Borden

# Off to First Grade

illustrated by **Joan Rankin**

Margaret K. McElderry Books
New York London Toronto Sydney

Margaret K. McElderry Books
An imprint of Simon & Schuster Children's Publishing Division
1230 Avenue of the Americas, New York, New York 10020
Text copyright © 2008 by Louise Borden
Illustrations copyright © 2008 by Joan Rankin
Book design by Krista Vossen
The text for this book is set in Triplex.
The illustrations for this book are rendered in watercolor.
Manufactured in China
10 9 8 7 6 5 4 3 2 1
Library of Congress Cataloging-in-Publication Data
Borden, Louise.
Off to first grade / Louise Borden ; illustrated by Joan
Rankin.—1st ed.
p. cm.
Summary: Each member of a first-grade class, as well as their
teacher, principal, and a bus driver, expresses excitement,
worry, or hope as the first day of school begins.
ISBN-13: 978-0-689-87395-9
ISBN-10: 0-689-87395-6
[1. First day of school—Fiction. 2. Schools—Fiction.]
I. Rankin, Joan, ill. II. Title.
PZ7.B64827Fi 2008
[E]—dc22
2005002320

For Abigail, our sunshine—L. B.
Especially for Jade—J. R.

# Anna

At last,
it is August 26th
on our calendar.
It's a big day!
The day
that I start first grade
at Elm School.
Mrs. Miller will be my teacher.

At breakfast
I tell my little brother, Ray,
about the zillions of books
I will bring home
to read to him.

# Ben

I look in the mirror
in our bathroom.
Then I tuck in my shirt
and stand as tall as I can.

"Good luck,
Mr. Handsome First Grader!"
My mom gives me
a big off-to-first-grade hug.

# Claire

My dad stands in our yard
and holds up his camera.

"Say *cheese*!" he calls
to me and my brother, C. J.

C. J. and I grin our best grins.
But I don't say cheese.
Instead I say:
"First grade!"

*Click!* goes the camera.

# Dee

The sun is up
and the sky is blue.
My mom says
it's perfect first grade weather.
We wait and wait
on the street corner
for the big yellow school bus.

At last!
I hear a *rmmm . . . rmmm*
coming up our street.
We look at the number on the bus.
It's number 5.
That's my bus!

I hug my mom good-bye,
and I'm off to first grade.

# Erik, Felicia, and Gabby

All three of us are on Bus 19.
We are off to first grade,
and Mrs. Miller will be our teacher.
Our bus makes seven more stops
on the way to Elm School.

On the bus
Erik tells us
that Mrs. Miller is nice
and that she puts on a black top hat
during math class
and does magic tricks
with a handkerchief and dimes.
Erik's sister was in Mrs. Miller's class
last year,
so Erik knows
all the important
first grade stuff.

**A top hat!**

We will be math magicians!

# Henry

I'm on Bus 3,
and I have a box of new
markers
and a box of new crayons
in my backpack.

My grandma says
I'm the artist in the family.
I have a *huge* paint box
at home.

A third grader
sits next to me
on Bus 3.
She says Mrs. Miller
has clay
*and* paper
*and* brushes
*and* paint
in her classroom.
I can't *wait*
to be a first grade artist.

# Ignacio

I am in a new country:
America.

My school is new to me
too.
My papa works in a new job.
He says many people
who are immigrants
have come to America.
Just like us.

Last week
we met Mrs. Miller,
my teacher,
and Mr. Zimmerman,
my principal.
They told me
they would help me
with my English.

Today is my first day.
I hold my papa's hand
and practice my English.
*Elm School.*
*Mrs. Miller.*
*First grade.*

# Josh, Kristen, and Li

We're on Bus 9,
and we will be first graders
in Mrs. Miller's class.

All three of us like sports.
Our favorite sports are

basketball and baseball . . .

hockey and lacrosse . . .

football and swimming.

Elm School is a new school
for Li.
He went to kindergarten
at another school.
Kristen tells Li:
"Don't worry.
You'll like the kids
at Elm School.
Josh and I will be
your first friends.
We're on your team!"

Felicia  Erik  Dee  Claire  Ben  Anna

Gabby

Henry

# Mrs. Miller

Ignacio

Josh

It's the first day of school.
My classroom is all ready
for my students.

I have asked Mr. Zimmerman,
our principal,
to visit our classroom
after lunch today.
I told Mr. Zimmerman:
"This will be my best class of readers yet!"

Kristen

Li

Nina

Last week I cut out twenty-three name tags,
*snip . . . snip . . . snip,*
one for each first grader's desk.

Otto

Polly

Today,
just before my students arrive,
I'll check those name tags,
one by one.
I want to remember all twenty-three names.

Quinn

Ramon

Shelley  Theo  Umberto  Victoria  Whit  Yoshi

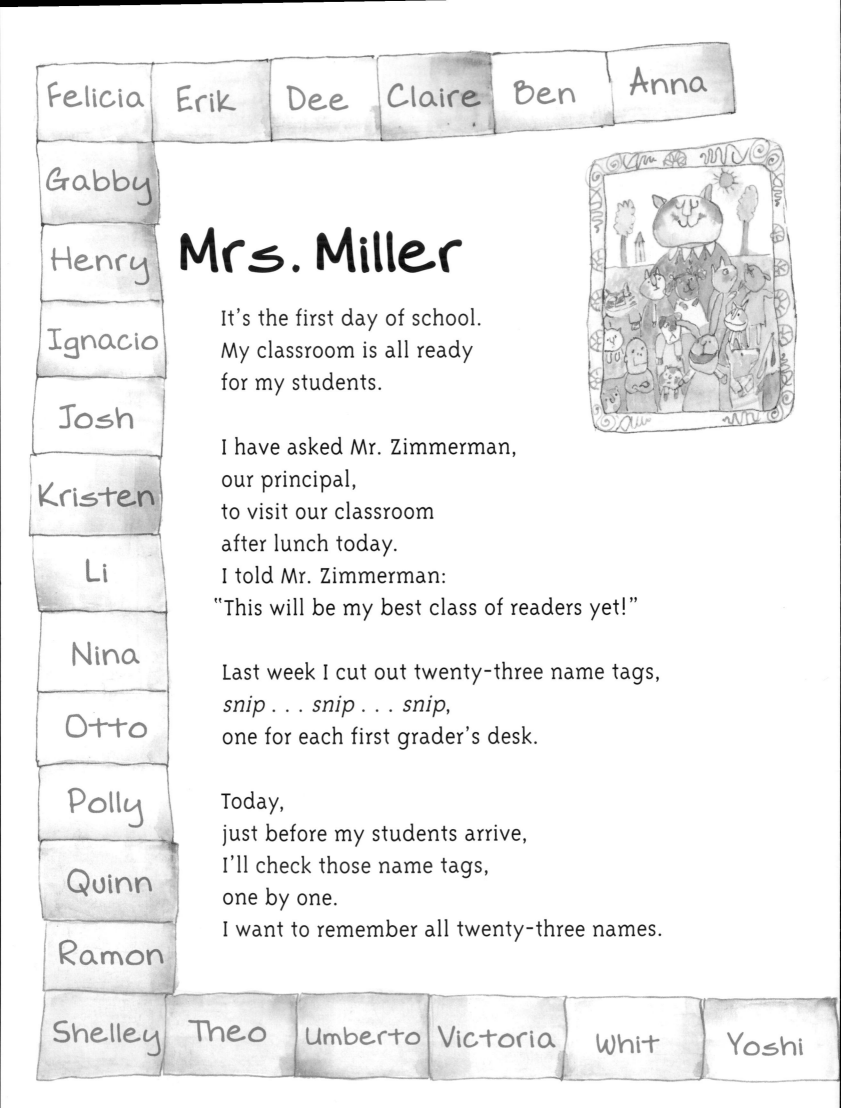

# Nina

My house is a block
from Elm School,
and today I'm off to first grade!

My grandpa Pops lives in Chicago
and he is here for a visit,
so I ask him to walk me to school.
My grandpa has gray hair,
and he likes to whistle songs.
He tells me he can remember
*his* first day
in first grade
sixty years ago.
We figure out his age together.
*Wow!*
Pops is pretty old!

When we get to the front doors
of my school,
I give Pops a hug.
I tell my grandpa
I'll always remember my first day
in first grade too.

# Otto

On the way to first grade
at Elm School,
I think about my grandma.

On Saturday
she bought me
new red sneakers.
Brand-new!
Not like those smelly hand-me-down sneakers
from my brother.

When Grandma told me red sneakers
were just right
for first grade,
I told Grandma
*she* was just right
for me.

# Polly

My mom hands me
a shiny new penny
to put in my pocket.
"For good luck in first grade!"

I hug her good-bye
and walk to Elm School
with my two big brothers.
They hold my hand as we cross the street.

I will show my penny to Mrs. Miller.
She'll be my teacher this year.
I keep my hand in my pocket,
holding my penny,
all the way to first grade.

# Quinn

My dad will take me to school today,
just like he did last year
when I was in kindergarten.

We listen to jazz music
on the radio in Dad's car
all the way to Elm School.

The sun is too bright in my eyes,
but I don't mind one little bit
because the windows are down
and I'm with my dad,
and I'm rap-tap-tapping my feet
to the beat.

My dad says jazz
is the best kind of music . . .
that there isn't any other music
like it.

I wonder if Mrs. Miller likes jazz.
I'll ask her today
when I get to first grade.

# Ramon

Mrs. Miller's classroom
is down a long hall.
But there are two long halls
in Elm School.

"Remember to turn right,
not left,"
my sister Lucia tells me
at the front doors of Elm School.

Lucia is in fifth grade.
Her classroom is upstairs.

Lots of kids hurry past us.
My sister gets a blue marker
out of her backpack.
She puts a big blue dot
on my right hand . . .
so I will turn right
and not left.

Lucia is the best sister
in the world.

# Shelley

My mom and my sister, Em,
walk me to school.

I push Em in her stroller
and hum a little song for her.
I call it Em's song.

At the front door of Elm School
I tell Em she is too little
to go with me to first grade.

Then I kiss her
and hug my mom,
and say good-bye
*three times*.

I hum Em's song
all the way down the long hall
to Mrs. Miller's classroom.

MRS. MILLER

← HERE

# Theo, Umberto, and Victoria

We're neighbors,
so we will walk to Elm School
together.

On the way
we stop and check our lunch boxes.
We lift the lids
and peek inside.

Theo has a tuna sandwich
and Umberto has ham.

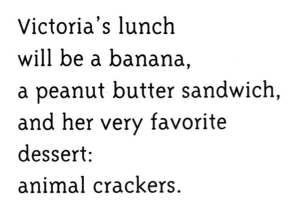

Victoria's lunch
will be a banana,
a peanut butter sandwich,
and her very favorite
dessert:
animal crackers.

Yum! Yum!

# Whit

I wonder
if Mrs. Miller is as nice
as my kindergarten teacher.

I wonder
if I will get to work
at a computer.

I wonder
if I'll get to write with chalk
on the big blackboard.

I wonder
if I will learn to read the words
in our first grade books.

I wonder
how I will know which desk
is my desk.

# Xavier

I drive Bus 3,
and I tell all the students
on my bus
to call me by my first name:
Xavier.

I tell kids I'm like Superman:
I have X-ray vision on my bus.
I can see monkey business
before it even happens.

The first day of school
is always terrific!
It's a new beginning
for all of us.

# Yoshi

Today is the first day
of first grade.
I wish I was going
back to kindergarten.
But I don't tell my dad.

On the way to Elm School
I tell my dad
I think first grade
should start *tomorrow*,
not today.

My dad says:
"Okay . . .
I'll ask Mr. Zimmerman
if you can go to *second grade* today . . .
and start first grade tomorrow."

I tell my dad
maybe today *is* a good day
to start first grade.

# Mr. Zimmerman

I'm the principal
at Elm School,
and I'm the luckiest person
in the world.

I talk with parents.
I read books to kids.
I play football
with the students at recess.

Today everyone at Elm School
gets an A⁺.
We're all ready to begin
the *best* school year ever.

*Hmm.*
Which book would be
just right
to read to Mrs. Miller's class
after lunch?